Where Are Meadow's Manners?

By Peta-Gaye Nash

Illustrated by Anindita Modak

. . . .

This Book is Dedicated to

Meadow,Chloe and Shiloh - *P.N.*
Maa, Baba, Sanjib and my bro John - *A.M.*

. . . .

Published by

"Mommy, get my breakfast!"

Oh-oh. Meadow didn't say please. Say please, Meadow.

Meadow shook her head.

"No." She said it again, even louder this time.

"Mommy! Get my breakfast NOW."

I think Meadow has lost her manners.

"Where have your manners gone?" asked Mommy. Meadow didn't know. "Meadow, your manners have gone out the window. Your manners have gone through the door."

Then when Meadow got her breakfast, she didn't say 'thank you.'

Throughout the day it seemed as if Meadow's manners had disappeared.

She broke her brother's Spiderman toy and she didn't say she was sorry.

She took her sister's cell phone and pressed all the buttons. Then she dropped the phone in the bathtub when it was filled with water.

 "Oh no, Meadow, you've ruined my phone."

Meadow didn't say she was sorry for that either.

Then, when she was playing a board game with her brother and she lost the game, she lost her temper and threw all the game pieces on the floor.

"I'm never playing with you again," she told her brother angrily.

Meadow even told her daddy that she didn't love him anymore and she told her mommy that she was going to put her in jail. I think Meadow really has to find her manners.

"Where did 'please' and 'thank you' go?" asked Mommy. "Is it under the pillow?"

Meadow shook her head.

"Did 'please' and 'thank you' go under the bed?" Meadow shook her head. Everyone tried to help Meadow find her manners.

"I think Meadow's manners are in the garden," said her brother. "I think the groundhog that ate all the lettuce in our garden is the one that took Meadow's manners and he's buried them underground. Meadow might not get her manners back until next year when he comes out on Groundhog Day."

Meadow's mom and dad went into the garden to search for the groundhog. The groundhog was sitting in a patch of sweet lemon balm plants, but he didn't have Meadow's manners. He said the only thing he had was a sore foot because the dog next door had chased him all morning.

"The squirrel has Meadow's manners. He's hidden them with all the nuts he's collected for the winter. I'm sure if we find the squirrel we'll also find 'please' and 'thank you'," said Mommy.

The squirrel was sitting on a branch in the plum tree.

"Squirrel, did you take Meadow's manners? She's lost 'please' and 'thank you' and 'I'm sorry'."

"I don't collect manners, only nuts and food for the winter."

The squirrel turned and scampered even higher up the tree.

"The sneaky raccoon must have Meadow's manners," said Daddy.

Shortly after dark, they went outside to ask the raccoon if she had Meadow's manners. They saw her lumbering towards the compost bin. She turned to face them and stood up on her two hind legs.

"I don't have 'please' and 'thank you' or 'I'm sorry'," said the raccoon, "but I do have some of your leftover sandwiches."

"No thank you, Mrs. Raccoon, we're only interested in getting Meadow's manners back."

The family searched high and low but it seemed that Meadow's manners had gone forever, because that evening she called her brother 'stinky face' and she refused to pick up her toys from the floor.

"I think the possum has Meadow's manners. We should go ask her," said Meadow's brother.

The possum was hanging upside down from a tree branch.

"Mrs. Possum, do you have Meadow's manners?"

"No, I don't," said the possum. "Do you have a map? I think I'm lost and I'm trying to find my way home."

"Where do you live?"

"Very far south," said the possum jumping down to the ground, "I really have to go now."

And saying that she ran off.

"I'm sure it's the blue jay that has Meadow's manners. She's taken them up to the birdhouse," said Meadow's sister.

The family looked in the birdhouse. They didn't find Meadow's manners, but they did find something very special.

"Congratulations on your babies, mommy bird."

Then something amazing happened.

"Mommy, can I please have a glass of water?" asked Meadow.

When Meadow got the glass of water, she said, "thank you."

"Wow! Meadow, you've found your manners. The groundhog didn't take them after all. The squirrel and the raccoon didn't take them. The possum and the blue jay didn't take them either. You had them all along," said Mommy excitedly.

Then Meadow cleaned up her toys, told her brother she was sorry for breaking his toy, and told her mom and dad she loved them. She even offered her sister her toy cell phone.

And later that night, she went to bed when it was bedtime. Everyone was glad that Meadow had finally found her manners.

I hope she remembers to use them when she wakes up tomorrow.